S0-BRT-445

POOH GOES
VISITING

A. A. MILNE

Pooh Goes Visiting

adapted by Stephen Krensky

with decorations by Ernest H. Shepard

Puffin Books

PUFFIN BOOKS
Published by the Penguin Group
Penguin Putnam Books for Young Readers, 345 Hudson Street, New York, New York 10014, U.S.A.
Penguin Books Ltd, 80 Strand, London WC2R ORL, England
Penguin Books Australia Ltd, Ringwood, Victoria, Australia
Penguin Books Canada Ltd, 10 Alcorn Avenue, Toronto, Ontario, Canada M4V 3B2
Penguin Books (N.Z.) Ltd, 182-190 Wairau Road, Auckland 10, New Zealand

Penguin Books Ltd, Registered Offices: Harmondsworth, Middlesex, England

First published in the United States of America by Dutton Children's Books and Puffin Books,
divisions of Penguin Putnam Books for Young Readers, 2002

1 3 5 7 9 10 8 6 4 2

Puffin Easy-to-Read ISBN 0-14-230184-1
Puffin® and Easy-to-Read® are registered trademarks of Penguin Putnam Inc.

Printed in China

Reading Level 2.2

8020

CONTENTS

1

POOH STEPS OUT

Winnie-the-Pooh was walking

through the forest one day,

humming proudly to himself.

He had made up a little hum

that very morning,

as he was doing his Stoutness Exercises.

"Tra-la-la, tra-la-la," he said,

stretching up as high as he could go.

And then *"Tra-la-la, tra-la—oh, help!—la,"*

as he tried to reach his toes.

He had said the hum over and over

until he had learned it by heart.

Now he was humming it

right through, properly.

Tra-la-la, tra-la-la,

Tra-la-la, tra-la-la,

Rum-tum-tiddle-um-tum.

Tiddle-iddle, tiddle-iddle,

Tiddle-iddle, tiddle-iddle,

Rum-tum-tum-tiddle-um.

Well, he was humming this hum,

when suddenly he came to a sandy bank.

And in the bank was a large hole.

"Aha!" said Pooh.

"If I know anything about anything,

that hole means Rabbit.

And Rabbit means Company.

And Company means Food."

So he bent down

and put his head into the hole.

"Is anybody at home?" he called out.

There was a scuffling noise

from inside the hole,

and then silence.

"What I said was,

'Is anybody at home?'"

called out Pooh very loudly.

"No!" said a voice.

"Bother!" said Pooh.

"Isn't there anybody here at all?"

"Nobody."

Pooh took his head out of the hole
and thought for a little.

"There must be somebody there,

because somebody must have *said*

'Nobody.'"

So he put his head back into the hole.

"Hallo, Rabbit, isn't that you?" he said.

"No," said Rabbit in a different sort of voice.

"But isn't that Rabbit's voice?" Pooh asked.

"I don't *think* so," said Rabbit.

"It isn't *meant* to be."

"Oh!" said Pooh.

He took his head out of the hole

and had another think.

Then he put it back in.

"Well," he said,

"could you very kindly

tell me where Rabbit is?"

"He has gone to see his friend

Pooh Bear," said Rabbit.

"But this *is* Me!" said Bear,

very much surprised.

"What sort of Me?" asked Rabbit.

"Pooh Bear."

"Are you sure?" said Rabbit.

"Quite, quite sure," said Pooh.

"Oh, well, then," said Rabbit,

"come in."

2

POOH HAS A LITTLE SOMETHING

So Pooh pushed and pushed and pushed his way through the hole, and at last he got in.

"You were quite right," said Rabbit, looking at him all over.

"It *is* you."

"Who did you think it was?" said Pooh.

"Well, I wasn't sure," said Rabbit.

"You know how it is in the forest.

One has to be *careful*.

What about a mouthful of something?"

Pooh always liked a little something

at eleven o'clock in the morning,

and he was very glad to see Rabbit

getting out the plates and mugs.

"Honey or condensed milk

with your bread?" asked Rabbit.

Pooh was so excited that he said, "Both."

And then, not wanting to seem greedy,

he added, "But don't bother

about the bread, please."

For a long time after that

he said nothing....

Until at last, humming to himself

in a rather sticky voice, he got up,

shook Rabbit lovingly by the paw,

and said that he must be going.

"Well, good-bye," said Rabbit.

"If you're sure you won't have

any more."

"*Is* there any more?" asked Pooh quickly.

Rabbit took the covers off the dishes.

"No, there isn't," he said.

"I thought not," said Pooh,

nodding to himself.

"Well, good-bye, then."

So Pooh started to climb

out of the hole.

He pulled with his front paws

and pushed with his back paws.

In a little while his nose

was out in the open again…

and then his ears…

and then his front paws…

and then his shoulders…

and then—

"Oh, help!" said Pooh.

"I'd better go back.

Oh, bother!" said Pooh.

"I shall have to go on.

I can't do either!" said Pooh.

"Oh, help *and* bother!"

3

POOH REMAINS IN A TIGHT PLACE

Now by this time

Rabbit wanted to go for a walk too.

Finding his front door full,

he went out the back,

and came round to Pooh.

"Hallo, are you stuck?"

he asked.

"N-no," said Pooh carelessly.

"Just resting and thinking

and humming to myself."

"Here, give us a paw," said Rabbit.

Pooh stretched out a paw,

and Rabbit pulled and

pulled and pulled....

"Ow!" cried Pooh. "You're hurting."

"The fact is," said Rabbit,

"you're stuck."

"It all comes," said Pooh crossly,

"of not having front doors

big enough."

"It all comes," said Rabbit sternly,

"of eating too much.

I thought at the time—

only I didn't want

to say anything—

that one of us was eating

too much.

And I knew it wasn't *me*.

Well, well, I shall go and fetch

Christopher Robin."

Christopher Robin lived at the other

end of the forest.

When he came back with Rabbit,

he saw the front half of Pooh.

"Silly old Bear," he said,

in such a loving voice

that everybody felt

quite hopeful again.

"I was just beginning to think,"

said Pooh, sniffing slightly,

"that Rabbit might never be able

to use his front door again.

And I should *hate* that."

"So should I," said Rabbit.

"Use his front door again?"

said Christopher Robin.

"Of course he'll use

his front door again."

"Good," said Rabbit.

"If we can't pull you out, Pooh,"

said Christopher Robin,

"we might push you back."

Rabbit scratched

his whiskers thoughtfully.

He pointed out that,

once Pooh was pushed back,

he was back.

Of course, nobody was more glad

to see Pooh than *he* was.

Still, some lived in trees

and some lived underground, and—

"You mean I'd *never* get out?" said Pooh.

"I mean," said Rabbit,

"that having got *so* far,

it seems a pity to waste it."

Christopher Robin nodded.

"Then there's only one thing to be done,"

he said. "We shall have to wait

for you to get thin again."

"How long does getting thin take?"

asked Pooh anxiously.

"About a week, I should think,"

said Christopher Robin.

"But I can't stay here for a *week!*"

said Pooh.

"You can *stay* here all right,

silly old Bear,"

said Christopher Robin.

"It's getting you out which is

so difficult."

"We'll read to you," said Rabbit cheerfully.

"And I hope it won't snow.

And I say, as you're taking up

a good deal of room,

do you mind if I use your back legs as

a towel-horse?

"Because, I mean, there they are—

doing nothing—

and it would be very convenient."

"A week!" said Pooh gloomily.

"What about meals?"

"I'm afraid no meals,"

said Christopher Robin,

"because of getting thinner quicker."

Pooh began to sigh,

and then found he couldn't

because he was so tightly stuck.

A tear rolled down his eye.

"Then," he said,

"would you read a Sustaining Book

that would help and comfort

a Wedged Bear in Great Tightness?"

"Of course," said Christopher Robin.

4

POOH REGAINS
HIS FREEDOM

So for a week

Christopher Robin read

at the North end of Pooh.

And Rabbit hung his washing

on the South end.

And in between Pooh felt himself

getting slenderer and slenderer.

At the end of the week

Christopher Robin said, *"Now!"*

He took hold of Pooh's front paws,

and Rabbit took hold

of Christopher Robin.

And all of Rabbit's friends and

relations took hold of Rabbit.

Then they all pulled together.…

For a long time Pooh only said

"Ow!"… and *"Oh!"*…

Then, all of a sudden, he said *"Pop!"*

just as if a cork

were coming out of a bottle.

And Christopher Robin and Rabbit

and all Rabbit's friends and relations

went head-over-heels backwards . . .

and on the top of them

came Winnie-the-Pooh—free!

So, with a nod of thanks to his friends,

Pooh went on with his walk

through the forest,

humming proudly to himself.

But Christopher Robin

looked after him lovingly,

and said to himself,

"Silly old Bear!"

Chicken Soup
for the Soul.

Have
a Little
Faith

Amy Newmark

CSS

Chicken Soup for the Soul, LLC
Cos Cob, CT

Chicken Soup for the Soul: Have a Little Faith
Amy Newmark

Published by Chicken Soup for the Soul, LLC www.chickensoup.com

Copyright ©2017 by Chicken Soup for the Soul, LLC. All Rights Reserved.

The publisher gratefully acknowledges the many publishers and individuals who granted Chicken Soup for the Soul permission to reprint the cited material.

Front cover, back cover, and interior illustration courtesy of iStockphoto.com/Pony-art.

Interior photo of Amy Newmark courtesy of Susan Morrow at SwickPix

Cover and Interior by Daniel Zaccari

ISBN: 978-1-61159-059-3

PRINTED IN THE UNITED STATES OF AMERICA
on acid∞free paper

25 24 23 22 21 20 19 18 17   01 02 03 04 05 06 07 08 09 10 11

Table of Contents

Give Thanks

Music's the medicine of the mind.
~John A. Logan

The sounds of the helicopter blades were deafening, but all I could hear in my heart and soul was myself singing "Give thanks with a grateful heart." Just hours before I had crawled away from a fiery inferno that once was our motor home. I had seen my skin melting off my arms and legs and felt excruciating pain from my back. The intense heat was literally melting me. The black billowing smoke blinded me as I looked for my husband and daughter. As I raced from the menacing flames I screamed, "Save my family! Save my family!"

Now, as I lingered in a fog, lying on a stretcher, all I could remember is the song that I was singing. I had been taken by ambulance to a nearby hospital to be stabilized. I was told that my family was alive. The nurses quickly cut the clothes off my charred body and the wedding ring off my swollen finger. I could hear my adult daughter screaming, "I want my mother" over and over from the room next to mine. I kept insisting that I needed to be with her, but three people working on me held me down. I had no idea how extreme my injuries were, and my heart was breaking with each one of her screams. They calmly kept telling me she was all right, and that they had taken my husband by helicopter to the burn center three hours away. That is when the song started playing in my head. My family is alive, and all I wanted to do was to praise God.

Now I was in the helicopter on my way to the burn center. "Give thanks with a grateful heart, give thanks to the Holy One, give thanks for what He has done for me." As they lifted me off the helicopter, one of my good friends was there to greet me. I was trying to lift my hands as I sang, and she gently helped me as she joined in. I kept saying "God is good." He kept us all alive.

That song kept me going through my darkest hours. Several days passed, and when I woke up in the burn unit, I recognized the enormity of the accident. Forty-eight percent of my body was burned and my back had been broken. Our daughter was thrown through the window away from the fire but broke many bones. My husband was lying in a coma two rooms from my own. He had fifteen fractures in his head and was sixty-eight percent burned with a nine percent chance of living.

I was trapped inside a severely burned body and the pain was ferocious. I had in fact become a prisoner within my uncontrollable shivering frame. Tears poured from my eyes, but my burned arms and hands could not reach to wipe them away.

My entire life had been full of challenges, and I

knew my faith and music had always upheld me in the past. This time I would have to trust and allow them to carry me through this healing and restoring season. I had my son bring in a CD player and my praise worship music. The music played all through the day and gave me encouragement.

The song "Give Thanks" became my theme song for my bandage changes. Each day was full of extreme pain as I experienced two-hour bandage changes each morning and each night. I would ask my nurses to put my music on. As I tried to sing along, I would concentrate on each word, and the words would give me the hope I needed to get through. The nurses would sing along as they worked on me, and I found the music helped me with the pain management. Whenever I thought I could not go through another minute of the procedure, I would relocate into my music.

The melodies played on through the challenging and happy times of my life.

Thankfully, my husband and daughter survived.

I now sing happy songs to my grandchildren and life can't get much better. We've since made it our melody to share our success story with burn survivors and families all over the world, passing on the song of hope. I hope you too will find a song within the deep recesses of yourself to make it through life's challenging moments, knowing whatever your trial may be there is a brighter note to be sung.

~*Susan Lugli*

A True Friend, a Godsend

Two are better than one… For if they fall,
the one will lift up his fellow.
~Ecclesiastes

Not so long ago I was going through a real difficult time in my life that truly I could not have faced alone. Up until this point in life, I felt that I was finally getting a handle on things and was making some progress. My mindset was geared toward achieving success for the sake of my family. You see, I had all of my priorities wrong. I measured success in life based upon the amount of money I earned, the position

I held, and the things I could afford for my family. I always thought that I was doing it for them. But then one day my wife walked out on me, taking our son with her. Two weeks later I lost my job; eventually I lost our home, car, and everything else I had worked so hard to attain. In desperation I called out to God, but it seemed I couldn't get an answer.

For days, weeks, and months, I cried and prayed, asking God "Why are these things happening to me? Lord, I have been faithful in attending church, tithing, and living a Godly life to the best of my understanding. So why am I experiencing the trouble I suddenly find myself facing?"

I have never had many friends who I could call true, close friends. Most were just social friends who I would go to lunch with on Sundays after morning service. Some would occasionally stop by our place, but usually this was only if we had invited them over for supper. But we never had someone who would just stop in to say, "Hi, are you okay?

Are things going well? Haven't heard from you in a day or two and felt I needed to check on you."

However, a couple of years before this crisis, while working as the manager of a local bookstore, I met a gentleman who was interested in selling his book on consignment. So after reviewing his book, we accepted it. Over the next couple of months, Sam came by on several occasions to check on his book. Since it was his first book to be published, he was eager to make a sale. Each time he stopped by, we would talk about his writing and I would do my best to give him my insight on different publishers. During these conversations a friendship was born. At one point we began having lunch together. And over a period of a couple of years, our friendship developed to the point that we would confide in each other about things that were happening in our personal lives.

I didn't realize it at the time, but God was preparing me for what I was about to face later on. After my wife left, I was alone. I never had a strong relationship with my mother, brother, or sister. I love them, and we talked occasionally, but we did not have that close bond so that I could confide in them about my situation. But I had Sam. He would stop by on a regular basis just to check on me. At times he would bring food, or ask me to go to a restaurant with him. Of course, being unemployed I didn't have the funds to eat out, but he insisted that I go with him and that he would pay for it. He told me many times, "Don't worry about it. I enjoy the friendship and fellowship." Being a prideful person, I sometimes found it difficult to say yes. I felt that if I couldn't pay my own way, then I shouldn't be going. But God was teaching me a lesson in humility.

On several occasions I would get the blues and start feeling lonely. Then in prayer I would question, "God, why am I faced with this trial? I feel so alone." At times, I didn't have a dollar to my name and no gas in the car to go searching for a job. I had been unemployed for a couple of months. But then Sam would drop by and before leaving he would reach into his pocket and say, "I just felt that I should give you this." And he would stick money into my shirt pocket. In my stubborn prideful way, I wanted to say "No thanks!" But in reality, I truly needed it and was thankful.

What I didn't understand for some time was that God was caring for me through Sam. Sam was more than just someone who stopped by now and then. There were nights that he would sit and patiently listen to my sob story, while I whined and complained. Then he would give me some words of encouragement and advice. There were times when I was so frustrated that I couldn't focus on what I needed to do in order to find a job. He would sit down at my computer and spend two or three hours doing job searches online and submitting my résumé for me. I didn't have the motivation to do it. I had hit rock bottom. I had just about given up.

One evening in prayer, as I began to meditate and listen to God, he reminded me of a scripture in the Bible found in 1 Kings 17 verses 1-6. It says that

God sent the prophet Elijah to the brook Cherith to stay there for a while. He drank the water from the brook and God sent ravens to bring him bread and meat every morning and night. That is when I got a clearer revelation about what was happening in my life.

From the beginning I had questioned God as to whether I had done something, or failed to do something, that caused his judgment to be pronounced upon me. I felt that maybe this trial was a curse from God for some sin in my life that I had failed to repent of. But that was not the case at all! God was teaching me to trust him for whatever provisions I needed for each day. He was teaching me that I couldn't stand alone as an Island, but that as a part of the body of Christ I need others to stand with me.

As for my daily sustenance, gas money, motivation, and encouragement, God sent my friend Sam on a regular basis. I thank Sam for being a true friend, and I thank God for the blessing of a true friend at a most crucial point in my life. It is my prayer that should I encounter someone who is in need of a friend, that I will be sensitive enough to recognize the need and humble enough to step up to the plate and fill that void in his or her life.

~Bob Arba

Blessed by More than Enough

All I have seen teaches me to trust the
Creator for all I have not seen.
~Ralph Waldo Emerson

The question was simple enough. "Do we have enough money to…?" My husband, Bob, asked that question each time he went to the store or filled up the truck with gas. It wasn't his question that put a huge knot in the middle of my stomach, but the answer I might have to give him.

Almost immediately after he purchased his dream truck the gas prices started to escalate. The new truck payment was a stretch for us. The higher gas prices and the rate at which this new vehicle drank the fuel was a potential budget breaker. It had already eaten the extra Bob allowed me to give to the church and was fast encroaching on what we considered staples of our lifestyle. The last fill-up cost sixty dollars. In a week the shiny red beauty would require another.

Because Bob was the only one making money, I felt guilt and shame when I had to tell him, no, we didn't have enough money in the bank for him to do something. His work schedule fluctuated, so if I did go to work the typical 8:00 to 5:00 office hours, we would not see each other. Neither of us wanted that. I stayed busy at home to compensate for my lack of earning power, but it was getting harder to justify staying home. Worse, the job market was dwindling while the gas prices soared.

Most days I checked the classifieds. I sent out résumés. I responded to interviews when I got a call. I did everything I knew to be a help to my husband. It seemed no one wanted me to work for them. I prayed for God to direct me.

One morning, in April of 2007, I sat down to read my Bible. It had opened to the fourteenth chapter of Matthew where Jesus fed a multitude of hungry people. He asked the disciples to take account of what they had. They tallied five loaves of bread and two fish—to feed five thousand men, not counting women and children. Matthew says Jesus looked toward Heaven and blessed the food. On another occasion, in the fifteenth chapter of Matthew, Jesus took the bread and the fish and gave thanks. He expressed gratitude for what he had.

What Jesus had was not enough. He didn't complain that it wasn't enough. There is no account written where he asked God for more. He took what he had, blessed it and gave thanks for it. Then he distributed it to those who had nothing and it was enough—no, it was more than enough. He got back twelve baskets more than he gave out.

I stopped reading and closed my eyes. I'd been

complaining. I told Bob with every fill-up that we needed to get rid of that pig of a truck. I hadn't been thankful we were still able to fill it up, but instead, I worried that we wouldn't be able to next time. That was a far cry from what Jesus did with what He had.

I opened my eyes and deliberately looked for reasons to be thankful. I began to bless the Lord for what we had. I thanked God that He provided for us all we needed, and even some things we didn't need—like Bob's truck. The more I blessed and thanked, the more peace reigned in my heart.

At lunch, I told Bob about my epiphany. "I believe we need to bless God and give thanks for all we have. That word bless means to speak well of. I believe we should display more gratitude for what we have."

He didn't say anything, just furrowed his brow and looked away while continuing to eat his lunch. But the peace in my heart assured me I was right.

I spent that afternoon speaking gratitude. I

blessed our family, our home—everything I could think of. I thanked God for his goodness toward us and his faithfulness. I went to bed that night feeling peace I hadn't felt in a long time.

The next morning I got a call from an acquaintance in the northern part of our state. Inez was part owner in a delivery service. They had an account with a bank located in the area where I live. The bank wanted to start a courier route in my area to service the banks in my town. Inez asked me to help her get it started.

I worked with her and the local bank to get the routes planned—all the day-to-day operations. She asked me to manage the route when we got the bid for it. I would be responsible for hiring employees, training, and scheduling. I took two of the routes myself and hired others to do the rest.

Without applying for a job, I had a job. I went from not having enough to having more than enough. This job was perfect for my husband's schedule. We could have dinner together every day. I was there when he got home from work and every weekend.

Inez blesses me continually — she's delighted with my work, and I in working with her. I praise the Lord for my job; I bless it and give thanks constantly. It is a miracle to me — a God-provision.

I know now, as I watch the jobless rate climb and our retirement plans dwindle, that God will provide. He has said he is willing. He has proven himself able. I refuse to worry.

My husband recently experienced deep cuts in his wages due to the economy. We now have an income substantially less than we had last month. But I continue to bless what we have and I am still so grateful for what God has provided. I take what we have and distribute it — and so far it has been enough. My trust is in God — not in the economy.

~Joie Fields

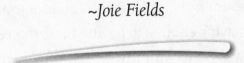

Lifestyle versus Life

I'm living my life, not buying a lifestyle.
~Barbara Kruger

The "perfect" lifestyle is never worth the cost of your life. If you have to sacrifice the quality of your family life or your spiritual life to keep up with your lifestyle ideals, you're cheating yourself. Society tells us if we just get that one more thing, we will be happy. Time after time, we give in only to find that we're still not really happy, so we go back to looking for that "one more thing."

One day two years ago, my husband, Scott, came home from work utterly depressed and burned out. The truth was that he'd been depressed for a couple of years. It is amazing what I could ignore in the busyness of our everyday lives. Just when you think you have everything together, life caves in on you. In all honesty, I panicked.

We lived in what I call "Stepford"—a very nice planned community for families. Little league under the lights, soccer fields, hiking trails, golf courses, you name it. We had a beautiful home, a great church, good schools for the kids, and a very comfortable lifestyle. We had the right cars, the right job, the right vacations. What we were lacking was a family life. Scott worked sixty to ninety hours a week. That's not a typo. That was our reality. He worked that crazy schedule for fifteen years. No wonder he was depressed.

Time isn't something you can ever earn back. Scott missed birthday parties and holidays and everything else in between for his career. I was raising our kids alone and also getting burned out—I wasn't doing it well, because I was doing it alone. In reality, our family didn't make a very pretty picture even though it was wrapped up in a beautiful package.

That month of our reckoning with reality, we faced some tough questions.

Is the time away from family worth the money Scott is making? If he quits his job, will we be able to provide for our four kids? When we began to talk about our current finances (which I was in charge of at the time), Scott asked me if I might have a gambling problem. "Of course not!" I said huffily. But then I realized the truth: our lifestyle was supported by credit cards. Our community was expensive. Keeping up with the Joneses never seemed to be at the forefront of our goals, but it certainly always lurked in the shadows.

We finally came to the same conclusion. Scott could not keep working at the same pace and survive. I could not keep raising our children alone and survive. What should we do? Tough questions require tough answers.

We prayed, our church prayed, our friends

prayed, and then we prayed some more. Then we made the tough decision: we would move back to Scott's home state and live with his mother until our house sold. He would look for a job that would support our new goal of working together to raise our kids and nourish our marriage.

We thought the process would take under six months; it actually took a year and a half. That's a long time to be in limbo — and I didn't like it at all. I got angry and stubborn and bitter. Why shouldn't I have a nice house? Why shouldn't we have nice clothes and a vacation and all those wonderful things? I still wanted my lifestyle. I liked the nice house, the pool, the golf course. There I was stuck in a house I didn't even own, with not one thing of my own around me — and for what?

Needless to say, that year was our stretching year. We were stretched, our marriage was stretched, our kids were stretched. But was the lifestyle we gave up worth the price of my marriage, my children's happiness, and my authentic happiness? I came to realize that the answer to this question was an easy one. No. Never.

The "perfect" lifestyle is never worth the cost of your life.

When we began to ask the tough questions and pray about what we knew would be tough answers, we began to put our priorities in order. But I had a lot to learn, and my heart didn't change overnight. I came to realize that while I may have been caring for my kids 24/7 all those years, I had also been selfish. In many ways, I had put my wants and needs above those of my family. To be selfish is to be human, but when I look back, I know I was most miserable while I was separating myself from God by prioritizing my lifestyle over the life He wanted for me.

In our new fish-out-of-water living arrangement, I finally picked up my dusty Bible and began to re-establish my faith life. Then I took a good hard look at my heart and chose to bloom where God had planted me. I began re-connecting with God.

While our circumstances haven't changed much, I am truly content. Our current "lifestyle" would be laughable by my old standards, but our family has never been closer — or more engaged in our faith lives.

I think I can sum it up with a conversation I had in the car one day with my fourteen-year-old son. I was trying to explain that while we didn't have as much "stuff" as we had in Arizona, his dad and I had made these decisions so that we could have a closer family. Tyler simply stated, "You know what, Mom? I think I saw Dad more in the first year we lived here than in the previous twelve years of my life."

That alone made every day of stretching ourselves worth it. The truth is, we may have given up everything we used to identify ourselves by, but what we got in exchange was priceless: we got our lives back.

~Kay Klebba

My Name
Is Nannymom

You don't choose your family. They are God's
gift to you, as you are to them.
~Desmond Tutu

When I turned forty, I went through some life-changing events.

My youngest child graduated from high school, my twenty-year marriage ended, I left my job as editor of a small newspaper, we had several deaths in my family, I moved twice, and I became a grandmother for the first time.

The announcement of the approaching baby

was not met with fanfare. My daughter would be a single mom and at the time my marriage was shaky to say the least. But when I saw the sonogram, heard the heartbeat, and felt this precious life move for the first time, my heart filled with joy.

God never makes mistakes.

I knew the birth of this child would be a blessing, and twelve years later, he is my gift.

When he was six months old, I began the journey of raising this child on my own. Well, not entirely on my own—God has always been there and my wonderful mother has stood by me through thick and thin.

Mimi says her reason for living is this boy. He is our joy. He has a loving spirit, a great sense of humor—much to his great-grandmother's dismay—is an honor roll student, loves church, fishing, playing computer games, building things, working puzzles, reading, and he is a big help to me at home and even at work.

I can't think of my life without him. Some people say it's not fair for me to have to raise this child, but I say it's an honor.

It hasn't always been easy. We've had to face some difficult situations, but my faith in God and His direction has always pulled me through.

This year I will turn fifty-three and my grandson will be thirteen—a teenager! Luckily, I can still keep up with him. I can ride go-carts, fly kites, play putt-putt, take long walks, camp, and take him on fun outings. I have some tough roads ahead and sometimes I do get scared—can I do this alone? But, then I remember I'm never alone. God is with me. I have my family, my church and many, many friends. This precious boy is my first priority when I'm at work, volunteering in my community, and at home. His contagious smile sincerely radiates his love for family and in the spur of a moment he is always willing to lend a hand.

My grandson calls me his nanny, and he knows

my daughter is his biological mother, but sometimes he simply refers to me as "Nannymom," and I wear that name with pride!

~Glenda Lee

God's Faithfulness

Faith is the virtue by which, clinging to the
faithfulness of God, we lean upon him, so that
we may obtain what he gives to us.
~William Ames

In the five years since my husband started working at the church we attend, he was rarely absent. He had a long commute five days a week. His work was mentally exhausting, but Joseph was happy. Then circumstances changed. My husband lost his job.

"I was sure God was preparing me for a future there. Now I'm no longer needed." Joseph's voice shook with emotion as he put his head in his hands.

Joseph's disappointment was keen and his spirit

crushed and he began to feel that God was displeased with him. This became a nagging and recurring thought.

Friends and co-workers from our church called to express their disappointment. He assisted them with their questions as they learned their new responsibilities in a changed environment.

"I've failed in some way or else I'd still be working there," he confided to me.

My husband's emotional wellbeing became as important as how we were going to manage financially, especially when he asked questions like, "What did I do wrong?" or "Now what?"

To get us through this crisis, I knew I needed God's help. I prayed for us. Then I began to see the hand of God in our situation.

We discovered that under the pension plan Joseph was enrolled in with a former employer, he could apply for early retirement benefits. This was our first indication that God was working on our behalf.

I've been a full time homemaker since our sons were born fifteen years ago. I decided to claim Social Security benefits this year when I reached age sixty-two. I learned at the time I applied that our boys were eligible for children's benefits as well. The Lord is faithful. He was providing for us.

A major concern was our children's education. It was re-enrollment time once again at their school. Would we be able to continue to provide them with the schooling we had committed to giving them? After applying for financial assistance, we were given a forty percent reduction on the following year's tuition. We were overjoyed!

And then there was the matter of health insurance coverage for us all. After some inquiries and searching the Internet, I learned that my husband and I were eligible for low-cost health insurance coverage. Our boys have free coverage under our state's children's health insurance program. God continued to meet our needs.

We now live more frugally on a lower, fixed

income. Fortunately, our home is mortgage-free. But the high cost of utilities was another concern. I applied for financial help with those costs and received discounts on our electric and heating bills.

Since my husband's unemployment, the blessings have been many. I felt disappointed that Ben and Tim only got to see their dad a short time each day when he worked full time at our church. Now their father sees them off to school in the morning and picks them up later. He is free to go on field trips and youth group outings. But most important, my husband now has the time to sit and talk with our boys. They are witnesses to God's faithfulness to our family during a time of crisis.

Until his employment ended, I was concerned about Joseph's long hours and how they were affecting his health. Now we spend time together during the day and he seems more relaxed.

"Maybe I could help at the school. Do they still need volunteers for grounds work?" Joseph asked our son recently. Many projects left unfinished at home are now getting completed, too.

I've seen my husband's disappointment gradually vanish. We are continually experiencing God's faithfulness and seeing new mercies in our changed situation.

I will continue to believe good things of God.

~*Pat Jeanne Davis*

Unexpected Blessings

Kindness, like a boomerang, always returns.
~Author Unknown

A few nights after Thanksgiving, my husband and I began planning the Christmas presents we would buy for our three boys. Money was tight, but thanks to careful budgeting we were in good shape. We couldn't wait for Christmas.

At 10:00 P.M., my husband answered a knock at the front door. There, standing in pajamas, were two neighborhood children, ten-year-old Andy and his seven-year-old sister, Beth. Tears streamed down their cheeks as they held a few wrapped Christmas gifts, an overstuffed pillowcase of dirty clothes resting on the cement beside them.

"M… Miss Kelley…" Andy said. "Can we stay with you?"

"What happened?"

"My dad and my aunt got into a fight and she kicked us out," Andy managed between sobs.

I looked into the darkness for their father. "Where's your dad?"

"He left. He told us to come here."

"Of course you can stay," I said, moving aside to let them in. It was late and they had school the next day. They could spend the night, go to school with my boys, and then I could figure out what was happening.

I woke my son and told him to go sleep in his brother's extra bunk bed. Then I put Andy and Beth into his bunk beds.

"Don't worry," I said. "Tomorrow I'll find out what's going on."

The next morning, after the kids left for the

bus, a knock sounded at the front door. It was Mr. Brown.

"Miss Kelley, I hate to trouble you, but can I come in and talk?" he asked politely.

"Please do." I moved aside for him to enter.

"I appreciate you letting Andy and Beth spend the night," he began. "My sister-in-law kicked us out. I didn't know where else to send the kids."

"How did you know they spent the night?" I asked, remembering that I saw no one last night.

"I was hiding in the bushes. I need to ask you another favor," he continued. "Can Andy and Beth stay here until I get on my feet?"

"How long are we talking about?" I was dumbfounded.

"A couple of months at most."

So many thoughts raced through my head. Christmas was in a few weeks. Money was already tight. We could barely afford the food and bills now. More kids meant more food, more water, more laundry soap, more bathing soap, more shampoo and toothpaste.

"I know it's a lot to ask," he said. "I don't know anyone here. Please let them stay. I don't want them to suffer because of my mistakes."

"Okay," I finally said. "The kids can stay. But ONLY the kids. You will need to stay at a shelter or something. But you can visit them. And this is just until you get on your feet."

"Thank you," he said. "You don't know how much I appreciate this." He promised to find a job quickly and work hard to get them a place to stay. "They have more clothes, but they're dirty."

I opened my garage, where the washer and dryer were and let him bring in the loaded pillowcases.

After he was gone, I cleared a dresser for them and placed their presents under the tree.

I wondered about Christmas. Was this all they had? I assumed it was, especially since Mr. Brown had no job. How could Santa visit my kids and not these two? He couldn't. I silently prayed that we would be able to afford a nice Christmas for everyone this year.

The phone rang. It was the school. Andy and Beth had talked with the guidance counselor and she wanted to know what was happening with the children. I told her what Mr. Brown had told me, and that the kids would be staying with me for a few months.

When the kids arrived home, I sat them all down in the living room to talk. Then I told Andy and Beth about our daily routine. "Directly after school, we always grab a snack and sit at the kitchen table to do our homework."

The new kids easily settled into our routine. Somehow we managed with food and daily supplies. But the bills hadn't come in yet. I was worried about how much more we would be paying. And with the extra money we spent on snacks and supplies like toilet paper and laundry soap, I wasn't sure we'd be able to pay them without taking money from our Christmas fund.

Two weeks later, the school called again. The

counselor asked what we were doing for Christmas.

"Good question," I said, laughing a little anxiously. "I'm not sure yet."

"Do Andy and Beth have Christmas presents?"

"They brought a few with them, but that's all they have," I said. "We don't have a lot of money, but Santa will come. I guess Christmas will just be smaller this year."

"We adopt families at Christmas," she said. "We would like to adopt Andy and Beth if that would be okay with you."

Silence.

"We already have people standing by to bring the gifts to your house. We have two bicycles and toys and clothes. You could put them away until Christmas."

"Okay." Inside I was silently thanking God. My boys wanted new bikes for Christmas too, but if we had to buy presents for Andy and Beth, we couldn't get them. We couldn't afford five bikes and we wanted everyone to have an equal Christmas.

Within a half hour, four cars pulled up and eight people began carrying in bags and boxes filled with gifts and food.

The phone rang again. It was another group that wanted to bring food. Just as the first group was leaving, the next group drove up with bags filled with food. My cupboards had never been so full.

After taking inventory, I hid the presents for Andy and Beth. That evening, my husband and I went shopping for our boys. We were able to get them everything they wanted and all the kids would be having a comparable Christmas. Our excitement returned.

But then the bills began arriving. I opened the water bill first. It was much lower than it had ever been. I stared at the paper thinking it must be some mistake, but silently thanked God for the blessing.

I opened the electric bill next. It was lower too. Even though we had used more, our bills reflected less. I knew that our holiday would be extra special this year.

It was. The kids awoke to a tree piled high with presents. We ate turkey and ham, potatoes and gravy, all sorts of vegetables, rolls, and deserts. Mr. Brown spent the day. And no one talked of anything sad. We played. We ate. And we thanked God for the blessings he bestowed on our two families.

Andy and Beth remained for two more months. And God continued to bless our home. We gave in our need and got more than we'd ever had before. We received love from a family that needed our help, we received joy from helping others, and we received faith that came from a shower of unexpected blessings.

~*Kelley Hunsicker*

The Blessing of a Friend

There is one word which may serve as a rule
of practice for all one's life — reciprocity.
~Confucius

For weeks on end, I waited to receive the call that I had lost my job due to cutbacks. Times were tough and I worked part-time at a private Christian school. All the employees were aware that problems in the economy had reduced enrollment. We were also aware that other local Christian schools had recently cut the number of classes and one had even closed. It was only a matter of time till I had no job at all.

When our school mentioned having to make cuts, such as not replacing some people who were leaving, freezing raises, and cutting non-essential personnel, I was sure I would be one of the first employees let go. After all, I had only been working at the school one year and shared a secretarial job with another woman who had been at the school many years. I worked the morning shift and she worked the afternoon shift. If they had to cut our position back to one person part-time, I was lowest on the totem pole. My husband and I loved the school and wanted our children to continue attending, but we knew it would be financially difficult, if not impossible, to keep three children there without me working.

All of our kids were well adjusted in the school and doing well academically. They were sharing with us the Bible lessons they were learning from their once a week chapel and from their daily Bible instruction in each of their classes. They had all made many friends, and the thought of making them change schools or become homeschooled again was unpleasant at best.

Because I was part-time I didn't work in the summer, but I checked in with the full-time people often to see how things were going. News was bad. Enrollment was not going up very fast. Jobs were being cut. Teachers lost their aides. Some grades went from two classes to one, so even some teachers lost their jobs. My income was not supporting the family but it did allow my children to attend. I prayed daily for those people at the school who needed their jobs to pay their bills and feed their families. But then I also prayed that my kids could keep attending. At the end of each prayer I prayed for God's will, knowing that He knows better than we do what we need.

The woman I job-shared with had worked at the school while her own children had attended, clear through to graduation. She was like a mentor to me. I often went to her with questions because she knew our position so much better than I did.

If I lost my job, I'd miss not only the income, but working with her and the other ladies in my office. But as I said earlier, I knew God would take care of my situation.

The call came. My position had been cut from two part-time people to one. I was prepared to walk away, but what I wasn't prepared for was that my job-share partner had voluntarily given up her job so that I could keep mine. God was working in a way I had not expected.

This wonderful woman blessed me and my family by helping my kids to stay at the school. On the phone one day she told me, "I wanted to give your kids the same chance to stay through graduation that my girls had."

Not only did this wonderful friend give up her job for me, but she now fills in whenever I need a day off. I have had to call her many times at the last minute because of sick kids or other needs and she has been right there to work for me. I pray good things for her often and tell her that she has been a huge blessing for my family during these tough times.

Ultimately it's God that helps us through the tough times. In many cases, like this one, it's evident how He does it. Through the sacrificial love of others.

~Angel Ford

Election Day Setback

*To succeed in life, you need three things: a
wishbone, a backbone and a funnybone.*
~Reba McEntire

I'd just driven away from my elderly client's
home late in the afternoon when I noticed
I had a missed call on my cell phone. It was
from my husband. "Uh-oh," I groaned. That
could mean only one thing. I waited until I arrived
home to call him back.

"Hi honey," I said as cheerfully as I could when
he answered. "Sorry I missed your call. What's up?"
I had a feeling down deep in my gut that I knew
what he was going to say. He'd been having trouble
at work for several months. Ever since a new set

of managers took over his department. Men who seemed bent on getting rid of him.

"It's over."

I think my heart stopped beating for a second or two. "It is?"

"Yep. I'm unemployed."

On that crisp November day—the same day Barack Obama made history by being elected the first black president of the United States—my husband was fired from a company he'd been with for more than twenty-three years. He'd worked there since he graduated from college. Since before we were married.

Somehow I didn't collapse in a puddle of tears right there on the kitchen floor. He certainly didn't need to deal with a hysterical wife. "Why don't you take some time to yourself before you come home," I suggested, knowing he probably wouldn't feel like facing the boys or me just then. He took me up on my offer and we hung up.

My heart was racing as I stared out the window

to the backyard. Anxious, angry thoughts whirled through my mind.

That stupid, stupid company! Those stupid, stupid people!

One person in particular came to mind. My husband's former supervisor was also a longtime friend. How could he have been involved in this? How could they fire my husband, without so much as a penny of severance? After twenty-three years of being a dependable, hard-working, trustworthy employee, this is what he gets? The whole thing was simply too surreal to fathom just then, yet there were some very real matters we needed to face.

Like telling our two teenage sons.

I called the boys into the living room. I thought it best to prepare them before my husband came home. He wouldn't exactly be in the mood to explain things in a calm, soothing manner.

"Boys," I said, taking a deep breath. "We need to talk."

They both stared at me. It was obvious they

knew something was wrong.

"Did Grandma die?" my fifteen-year-old asked, referring to my eighty-two-year-old mother who suffered from Alzheimer's disease and was not doing well.

I shook my head. "No, no. It's nothing like that." Although, in a way it was. The feelings and emotions that come with losing a job are very similar to those we experience when a death occurs. Sadness. Anger. Depression. Add to that the feelings of betrayal, and you've got a whopper of emotional baggage to sort through.

The boys kept staring at me. I decided to just blurt it out. "Dad was fired today."

Silence.

"We'll be okay," I reassured, knowing in my heart we would, but at the same time wondering how things would play out in the coming months. I work part-time. My husband was the main breadwinner. His job also provided our health and life insurance policies. What would we do now?

"Will we have to move?" Again, my youngest son, the worrier, voiced the question. My seventeen-year-old son, the one who rarely shows his emotions, stayed quiet. Much too quiet.

"No, we aren't going to have to move," came my firm, certain answer.

I hope not anyway, I worried silently, but who knows what might happen in the next few months. Our area hadn't suffered as many job losses as the rest of the country, but there are no guarantees when it comes to unemployment and securing a new job. I didn't share that concern with my sons though. There was no need to put unfounded fears on the table just yet. With both boys in high school, the prospect of moving was not something anyone in our family wanted. It made me sad they had to worry about such things now.

The tears came then. I hated to cry in front of the boys and I reined in the traitorous wetness fairly quickly, but it was obvious to them that I was worried. And hurt. But I also tried to be as optimistic as possible.

"Dad will find a new job. You know I've wanted him to leave that company for a while now. Maybe this is God's way of giving him something new. A better job. A job where he'll be appreciated."

With all my heart, I prayed that was true. The boys went back to their rooms and I waited for my husband to come home. When he walked in the door a short time later, I put on a brave smile to greet him. I even had some confetti to toss at him as he came into the kitchen.

"Hooray! Welcome home! You're free! Free! Free at last!"

He gave a slight chuckle. I'm sure he thinks he's married to a loon. "I'm free, all right. Free and unemployed."

Later that night we grew more serious. We talked about the immediate future and how we planned to make ends meet. We talked about résumés. We talked about the boys. We talked about all kinds of things.

And we prayed. God has a plan in all of this. Years down the road we'll look back and see how it all worked for our good. Right now, however, it didn't feel so good. It felt scary. Like being lost in a pitch-black cave without a flashlight. I don't like being scared, so I shoved thoughts of uncertainty away.

"Well," I said, trying to lighten the mood in the room. "Look at the bright side."

"What's that?" my husband asked.

"You don't have to get up at 4:45 A.M. anymore. You can sleep in!"

He actually smiled about that.

I found a few more things to add to the bright side list. He wouldn't have to eat leftovers for lunch every day. He'd save gallons and gallons of gas since he wouldn't have to commute into the city. And he'd be home a lot more, which was good for me and for the boys. He'd worked so hard for so many years, he'd missed a lot of time with the family. It would be nice to have him around.

"You know," I said as I gave him a big hug and settled in for the night. "I think I'm going to enjoy your unemployment. Just think of all the things you can do around the house while you're home. The yard needs some new mulch, and the trees need to be trimmed, and the bedroom ceiling needs to be repaired, and..."

He got the idea. "I hope I find a new job before you work me to death."

"Yeah," I grinned. "You will. But until then, you're all mine!"

~Michelle Shocklee

Drinking from Ola's Cup

Find yourself a cup of tea; the teapot is behind
you. Now tell me about hundreds of things.
~Saki

I t never failed. As I sipped the hot raspberry tea from the fragile china cup, I could almost see my sweet friend, Ola, sitting across the table once again. My fingers traced the delicate wildflowers painted on the cup she had given me. Once more, I was filled with gratefulness as I mulled over our unlikely friendship.

Ola was a tiny, frail wisp of a woman in her eighties who spent most of her time in a wheelchair.

Under ordinary circumstances we might not have become such close friends. I was a thirty-six-year-old mother of four children. Who would think we had much in common? But we shared a bond that drew us closer than most. We met at a grief support group that met every Monday night. Both of our husbands had died recently. We were both seeking relief from the deep pain that threatened to consume us.

Naturally, there was a lot of sorrow and weeping in our group. There were some whose spouse had died, some whose parents had recently passed away, and a few who were there because of the death of a child. Some had experienced a long lingering illness with their loved one, while others were going through the shock of a traumatic accident that had taken their loved one without warning. Needless to say, our meetings were filled with much pain and anguish. Our group was a place where others really understood what you were going through.

Some group members were quiet and withdrawn, barely holding back their emotions. There were those who wallowed in self-pity, repeatedly asking why this terrible thing had happened to them. A few regulars were like pressure cookers, their rage ready to blow at the slightest nudge. Then there was Ola.

Every week her daughter wheeled her into the room. There wasn't anything to make you sit up and take notice of Ola. She was just a tiny white-haired old lady in a wheelchair. Her physical frailties were deceiving, though. Inside that withered little body of hers lived a strong determined spirit. Each week revealed more of it.

For such a feeble thing, Ola had an outspoken personality. She was always ready to share a joke to lighten the grief. But she shared more. Her age gave her the right to offer us guidance and encouragement. We all listened, knowing she had survived many hard times in her life. She and her four children had been abandoned by her first husband. After she married again, she discovered her second husband was an alcoholic. Later he was in an explosion which left him severely deformed. Two of her children died at an early age.

One thing she shared with us stood out above everything else. In a group of people whose lives were devastated, Ola consistently reminded us to think of things to be thankful for. She promised us that our hearts would be lifted if we did. Ola told us if we couldn't think of anything else, we should at least thank God for the air that we breathe. Through her wrinkled face glowed a light of wisdom and faith that had been born from a long and difficult journey. Before each meeting ended, Ola would begin thanking God for specific things. Some tried to follow her lead. It was amazing to see the hope in people's faces when they joined in.

Sadly, others were too angry or blinded by pain to think of anything to be thankful for. All they could see was their own tragic heartache. They remained bitter and overwhelmed by their grief.

I chose to follow Ola's lead. If she could be thankful despite all her hard times, I could certainly try. My heart longed to feel the hope that I saw in Ola. At first it was difficult. My loss seemed so great, I didn't know if I would ever smile again. Though it was tempting to feel sorry for myself, I was determined to be grateful.

I decided to begin by thanking God for the wonderful gift of having Steve in my life for twenty years. I would have loved more years, but that's longer than what some people have. And what a great twenty years it had been! My mind wandered as I thought about what my life would have been like if I had not known him. Before long, sweet memories flooded over me giving me more reasons to thank God: the walks through fields of wildflowers, exploring old abandoned houses together, the soothing sounds of Steve's guitar filling the house every night.

Then I thought of our four children who depended on me. How empty my life would be without them. They would carry pieces of their dad throughout the rest of their lives. How grateful I was for each child and the time they got to spend with their dad.

I thanked God for my fifteen-year-old daughter, who had her dad's zest for adventure and his fun easygoing way with people. I thanked God for our oldest son, who had learned from his dad how to stand tall as a man of loyalty and responsibility. Then I thanked God for my quiet seven-year-old son who had seen more suffering through his dad's illness than most people see in a lifetime. I knew his deep compassion would be used in the future. Of course, I had to thank God for our two-year-old son who came as a total shock in the midst of acute emergencies and hospital stays.

Then I thought of all the doctors and nurses who had showed us such kindness during Steve's long illness. I also had to thank God for our friends and family who had given us gifts of time, money and prayers during the hard times.

As I thought of the difficult battle we had gone through with Steve's illness, I had to thank God for the strength that He had given us both. We had withstood something that was impossible to handle on our own.

Though I would miss my husband terribly, I had to thank God that he was finally free from the grip of daily suffering. I tried to imagine what it will be like some day when we are reunited in eternal life and I paused to thank God for the promise of that life to come which will be free from all sickness, death and hard times.

I suddenly realized that I was filled with a peaceful feeling of quiet joy! It had sprung from my grateful heart. My future shone brighter and full of hope. I knew I could go on. I knew I would never be alone. I felt so blessed!

My sweet friend Ola has since passed from this life. Every time I drink from the cup she gave me, I count my blessings. No matter what's going on, it's not long before I feel blessed beyond words. It has been said that a pessimist looks at his cup and sees it half empty, and that an optimist sees his cup half full. As I hold Ola's cup in my hands and find things to thank God for, I realize that my cup overflows!!

~Eva Juliuson

This Very Day

May you live every day of your life.
~Jonathan Swift

It would take many pages to explain the challenges my husband and I have faced. I have kept a journal for thirty years to help me keep my perspective. Recently I wrote this: Lord, this very day I awoke, alive, here, now — this day. This day I will treat my body with respect. Nourish it well, clean it, protect it. A warm shower, a healthy meal, fastening my seat belt, wearing comfortable shoes… these will be my little acts of respect for this body You gave me — this body You breathed life into at birth and each day including this very day.

This very day I awoke, not alone, but unique as I am, a part of all mankind, each single person also unique. Let me respect the body of humanity and treat each single member as well as I treat my hands, my face, my feet. As I nourish my body let me nourish also the greater body. As I pour milk on my breakfast cereal, let me remember also to pour the milk of kindness on my family, my neighbors and colleagues, the stranger in traffic and souls in distant lands with prayers of compassion and thoughts of understanding.

This very day Lord, I will no doubt feel grains of irritation. Let me, with my degrees, my skills, my "knowledge of life," not overlook the simple wisdom of the oyster. Let me turn those parasites that would invade my attitude with bitterness or despair into pearls to shimmer in my world, gems to offer others proof that life and hope can conquer depression and fear.

This very day Lord, let me remember to smile, to laugh, to sing, to dance, even if my knees hurt. Let me remember to watch the doves winging past my window, to see the coppery glint of sun on a squirrel's tail, to listen to the puppy lapping water from his dish. Let me notice the bright vermillion blossom in the ditch even if it is just a "weed." Let me be amused by bumper stickers on trucks decked in shiny chrome and fat backpacks on skinny teens. Let me, as I walk to the post office, be delighted by babies cooing in strollers and fussing matrons in flowered frocks and the aroma of hot cinnamon buns from the local bakery.

Since I am alive this very day, let me live it!

~Phyllis McKinley

Meet Our Contributors

Bob Arba was ordained a minister in 1997. He has been involved in Lay Ministry, Music Ministry and Youth Ministry for the past seventeen years. Bob enjoys playing music, reading, writing poetry and Christian fiction. Bob is working on his second fiction book. You may contact Bob at Arba2722@yahoo.com.

Pat Jeanne Davis is a homemaker and writer living in Philadelphia, PA with her husband and two sons. Her articles and short stories have appeared in regional and national publications. Pat has completed an historical inspirational novel. She can be reached at patjeannedavis@verizon.net or visit at www.patjeannedavis.com.

Joie Fields is author of the online BibleStudyNotes e-mail group at yahoo groups, as well as articles purchased by *Faith and Friends* and *War Cry* magazines and *Seasoned Cooking* e-zine. She and her husband, Bob, have two children and two grandchildren. They reside in Oklahoma.

Angel Ford is a wife and mother of three. She enjoys ministry, missions' related travel, spending time with her family and friends, and writing. She is currently working on a book and considering a master's degree. Please e-mail her at secretaryforhim@yahoo.com.

Kelley Hunsicker is a wife, mother, and grandmother, and in her spare time she writes from her home in South Carolina. Visit her at www.kelleyhunsicker.com.

Mother of seven, grandmother of nine, "prayer cheerleader" **Eva Juliuson** shares God's love through writing, teaching, and working with kids. For seven years, she's sent out short e-mail prayers to help jump-start others into a deeper personal prayer life with God. To receive them, you can e-mail her at evajuliuson@hotmail.com.

Kay Klebba is happily married to Scott and the mother of four incredible children including one with special needs. Kay's passion is speaking and writing to women about the hilarity of our blessings. Please visit her blog at http://kayklebba.blogspot.com or e-mail her at kayklebba@gmail.com.

Glenda Lee is an advertising director for a direct mail magazine. She is a published author of two bulletin board idea books, numerous magazine articles and poems. She enjoys writing, reading, gardening, fishing, spending time with her family and volunteer work. Please e-mail her at nanmom1@gmail.com.

Susan Lugli is a Christian speaker and author. Her stories have been published in *Chicken Soup for the Christian Woman's Soul*, *Chicken Soup for the Caregiver's Soul*, *Today's Christian Woman* magazine and many others. She is an advocate for burn survivors and speaks on their behalf. E-mail her at suenrusty@aol.com.

Phyllis McKinley has four books of poetry published and is the author of the children's book *Do Clouds Have Feet?* Her work has received multiple awards and has been published in Canada, the USA and the UK. She lives in southwest Florida with her husband Dr. Hanford Brace. You can e-mail her at leafybough@hotmail.com.

Michelle Shocklee lives with her family in Central Texas. She writes historical fiction and is a member of American Christian Fiction Writers. Michelle enjoys movie dates with her husband, laughing with her sons, and reading, especially research material for her novels. Visit her Blog at: michelleshocklee. blogspot.com.

Meet Amy Newmark

Amy Newmark is the best-selling author, editor-in-chief, and publisher of the *Chicken Soup for the Soul* book series. Since 2008, she has published 140 new books, most of them national bestsellers in the U.S. and Canada, more than doubling the number of Chicken Soup for the Soul titles in print today. She is also the author of *Simply Happy*, a crash course in Chicken Soup for the Soul advice and wisdom that is filled with easy-to-implement, practical tips for having a better life.

Amy is credited with revitalizing the Chicken Soup for the Soul brand, which has been a publishing industry phenomenon since the first book came out in 1993. By compiling inspirational and aspirational true stories curated from ordinary people who have had extraordinary experiences, Amy has kept the twenty-four-year-old Chicken Soup for the Soul brand fresh and relevant.

Amy graduated *magna cum laude* from Harvard University where she majored in Portuguese and minored in French. She then embarked on a three-decade career as a Wall Street analyst, a hedge fund manager, and a corporate executive in the technology field. She is a Chartered Financial Analyst.

Her return to literary pursuits was inevitable, as her honors thesis in college involved traveling throughout Brazil's impoverished northeast region, collecting stories from regular people. She is delighted to have come full circle in her writing career — from collecting stories "from the people" in Brazil as a twenty-year-old to, three decades later, collecting stories "from the people" for Chicken Soup for the Soul.

When Amy and her husband Bill, the CEO of Chicken Soup for the Soul, are not working, they are visiting their four grown children.

Follow Amy on Twitter @amynewmark. Listen to her free daily podcast, The Chicken Soup for the Soul Podcast, at www.chickensoup.podbean.com, or find it on iTunes, the Podcasts app on iPhone, or on your favorite podcast app on other devices.

Changing lives one story at a time®
www.chickensoup.com